Nelson in L♥ve

Also by Janice Lee Smith

The Monster in the Third Dresser Drawer
And Other Stories About Adam Joshua

The Kid Next Door and Other Headaches
More Stories About Adam Joshua

The Show-and-Tell War
And Other Stories About Adam Joshua

It's Not Easy Being George
Stories About Adam Joshua (And His Dog)

The Turkeys' Side of It
Adam Joshua's Thanksgiving

There's a Ghost in the Coatroom
Adam Joshua's Christmas

Nelson in Love

An Adam Joshua Valentine's Day Story

BY JANICE LEE SMITH
drawings by Dick Gackenbach

HarperCollins*Publishers*

Library of Congress Cataloging-in-Publication Data
Smith, Janice Lee, date
    Nelson in love: an Adam Joshua Valentine's Day story / by Janice Lee Smith;
drawings by Dick Gackenbach.
        p.   cm.
    Summary : Adam Joshua's Valentine's Day is extremely complicated and it
doesn't help matters to know his best friend Nelson and his dog George are
both in love.
    ISBN 0-06-020292-0. — ISBN 0-06-020293-9 (lib. bdg.)
    [1. Valentine's Day —Fiction. 2. Schools—Fiction. 3. Humorous stories.]
I. Gackenbach, Dick, ill.   II. Title.
PZ7.S6499Ne 1992   91-14667
[Fic]—dc20   CIP
                                                                     AC

DEDICATION

Our daughter was born ready to grasp life with both hands and her teeth. Scientific at age four, she experimented by wearing boots in her baths and dissecting all her dolls. Artistic at age six, she dazzled us with the beauty of her paintings, and we tried to overlook the fact that several were on walls. Creative at fourteen, she changed her name to Gypsy Jade and gave her heart to the theater forever.

Passionate about the world and its people, she protested injustice each time she met it, went broke spending her allowance on needy causes, gave unreserved love to countless friends, and kept always a shining certainty that she could make a difference.

She in turn baffled, bewildered, charmed, and enchanted us. And I joyously tried to capture her kaleidoscopic nature into the characters of Adam Joshua and his friends. Sometimes I felt glimmers of success, but always I felt the writing and the writer better for the inspiration.

Eighteen now, she's stepping out to take her place in the world. We hope the world is ready. We know it will be a far finer place when she's finished with it.

This is a thank you, Jaymi. Raising you has been one of life's great adventures. We wouldn't have missed it for anything.

Nelson in Love

CHAPTER 1

Everybody thought Halloween was the scary holiday, but Adam Joshua thought Valentine's Day was a whole lot scarier.

For instance, Adam Joshua had always thought there wasn't a surprise left in his best friend, Nelson.

But then one February morning on their walk to school, Nelson said, "Adam Joshua, have you ever noticed Heidi's hair?"

Actually, the only hair Adam Joshua ever noticed was his own when he had to brush it,

1

and George's. George got into an amazing number of things, even for a dog, and he usually had some pretty interesting stuff stuck in his fur.

"Heidi's hair is the neatest color in the sun," Nelson said, "and it's always really shiny and everything."

Adam Joshua stopped in the middle of the sidewalk to stare at Nelson, but Nelson kept right on walking and talking about Heidi's hair until Adam Joshua had to hurry to catch up.

"And it smells just great too," Nelson said with a sigh and a look in his eye that made Adam Joshua shiver clear down to his boots.

———

When Adam Joshua and Nelson walked into their classroom, a lot of people were busy doing a lot of things to get ready for Valentine's Day.

Some people were working on Valentine's

Day cards, and some people were working on the boxes for their cards to go into. Some people were sitting, staring glumly at unsigned cards, and unfinished boxes, and looking like they were sorry anybody had ever thought up Valentine's Day to begin with.

But since their teacher Ms. D. wasn't there yet to stop them, most people were lined up in front of Martha, getting ready to trade their milk money for a heart tattoo with initials in it.

"HEARTS BY MARTHA," Martha's sign said, and she had a lot of heart samples for display up and down her arms.

"Nobody really needs a heart," Angie said, coming over by the door to talk to Adam Joshua and Nelson, "but everybody thinks everybody else needs one, so everybody wants one."

Hanah handed Martha her money and stood there looking worried.

"I'm not sure I'm going to like this person forever," she said, rolling up her sleeve.

"Don't worry," Martha said. "With this marker, a tattoo only lasts through two baths."

"Great!" Hanah said, holding out her arm for Martha to begin. "I'll probably like him two baths long."

———

Heidi walked in the door and smiled at everyone, and Nelson turned into a Nelson that Adam Joshua had never seen before.

He turned several interesting colors, starting off with red and ending up at white, and then he stood there, with his knees shaking, mumbling down at his shoes.

He looked up grinning the minute Heidi had gone on past.

"Did you see that, Adam Joshua?" he asked happily, turning a normal Nelson color again. "Did you see what I mean about her hair?"

Ms. D. came bustling in the door with Mr. D. right behind, helping her bustle.

"Sorry to be running late," Ms. D. said, laughing and dumping a pile of books and papers on the desk. "Thanks for being so quiet."

"Pregnant people are very slow in the mornings," Mr. D. said, dumping another pile of books and papers beside the first.

"They're also slow in the afternoons, in the evenings, and in between," he said, chuckling. He helped Ms. D. off with her boots, kissed her on the nose, and headed for the door.

Martha caught him before he made it.

"It would be a nice way to say you care," Martha whispered, showing him her heart samples and her sign.

"Martha, no selling in class!" Ms. D. scolded.

Mr. D. and Martha both looked disappointed.

"Just as well," Mr. D. told Martha as he tried for the door again. "Ms. D. hardly ever gives me milk money anyway."

———

"I don't know," Angie said, putting her unsigned cards back in her desk as the class started settling down for the morning. "It seems to me Valentine's Day is an awfully lot of fuss for not very much candy or great gifts or anything."

A lot of people nodded their heads.

"I like to sign my valentines 'Guess Who?'" Angie said, "to make it more fun, but if everybody does that, then it's too many guesses to guess."

"How about signing them with a secret symbol?" Ms. D. said. "Something that shows something special about you, a clue, to make it easier and more fun to guess?"

Everybody got very quiet thinking about it for a minute, trying to decide if this was Ms. D.'s way of getting them into more work or if it really would be fun.

"Perfect," Angie finally said, and everybody nodded, satisfied.

———

All through the math and reading quiet times, Nelson kept his eye on Heidi and her hair, and Adam Joshua kept his eye on Nelson.

A lot of people kept their eyes on a lot of other people, but for the most part, nobody was ever looking at the person looking at them, so nobody's eyes ever met.

So many people sent Martha notes about needing hearts tattooed at recess, Martha started sending back numbers so everyone would know their place in line.

Adam Joshua couldn't wait to have quiet

time be over, so all the frenzy would quiet down.

Finally Ms. D. stood up, and that was getting to be such an interesting thing to watch, everybody gave her their full attention.

"I've had a great idea," she said, holding up a basket. "I think we need to work on appreciating each other this week."

Everyone looked suspicious. Ms. D.'s ideas weren't guaranteed, and this one didn't sound any too promising.

"From now until Valentine's Day, we're going to have 'Secret Friends.' Pick a strip of paper with a name on it," she said, holding the basket out to Angie, "and keep it a secret."

Angie started to pick a name, and then she stopped and looked scared.

"I understand the secret stuff," she said. "But does the 'friend' part mean *love* or anything?"

9

"Just *like*," Ms. D. said, chuckling. "I want you to leave secret notes, maybe even small gifts of candy or something, and tell that person what you like about them. Maybe you've seen them do something nice for someone, and you'd like to let them know. Maybe you just admire them, or you think they're great at doing things you wish you knew how to do."

Angie looked really nervous. She pulled a name out of the basket and looked at it.

"Thank goodness," Angie said. "She's nice and I can think of a lot of things I like about her."

All the rest of the girls in class started looking pleased and ready to get notes from Angie.

"Oh, yuck!" Philip said, choosing. "I can't believe I have to say nice things to this person. This person is a rat!"

A lot of people started looking worried,

and a lot of the rats kept their eyes down and didn't look at Philip.

There were a lot of *thank goodness*'s, and *oh, yuck*'s as Ms. D. passed the basket.

Actually, Adam Joshua didn't care who he got. He liked almost everybody in class, and he could think of something nice to say about nearly everyone.

Actually, there was only one person in the entire class he really, truly, absolutely, positively couldn't stand.

Actually, the only way he'd say "Oh, yuck!" was if he got that person.

"Adam Joshua," Ms. D. said, handing him the basket.

"Oh, yuck!" he moaned, reading the name on the slip.

———

Walking home with Nelson was worse than walking to school with him. Adam Joshua was used to Nelson talking all the time about his

11

fish, but he'd never known one person could find so much to say about another person's hair.

"You wouldn't believe the stuff that's happening out there," Adam Joshua told his dog, George, the minute he got home. "Everybody's going crazy."

George looked sorry to hear it.

"One of the worst things is that I think maybe Nelson's fallen in love," Adam Joshua said. "I mean with somebody other than a fish."

George looked amazed.

"And another worst thing is that the Secret Friend I have to appreciate is Elliot Banks. Elliot doesn't do anything that anybody could ever, ever appreciate."

George looked disgusted.

"Maybe Ms. D. appreciates him," Adam Joshua said. "But she doesn't always look as if she does. Maybe his mother appreciates

him, but I doubt it."

George looked doubtful about it himself.

"Anyway," Adam Joshua said, "a good thing was Ms. D.'s idea to use secret symbols on our valentines."

He got out his stack of valentines to get started.

"I'm going to use Superman's 'S,'" Adam Joshua said, showing George. "I've always wanted to use it and I don't think Superman would mind. But," Adam Joshua said, drawing a little more, "a lot of other people might use it, and Ms. D. said to give a clue to show something special about yourself, so . . .

"See?" Adam Joshua said, showing George the finished drawing of his symbol. "I drew your face in part of the 'S.' Everybody knows how special you are to me, so everybody should be able to guess."

George looked truly very honored, and deeply touched.

CHAPTER 2

Adam Joshua hugged George in bed the next morning as long as he could, and longer than George seemed to think was necessary.

It was just that in a world where even people like Nelson could change, it was nice to have a dog you could count on.

———

"Have you ever noticed that Heidi has dimples, Adam Joshua?" Nelson asked while they walked to school.

"I mean, I've never really noticed dimples

before," Nelson said, "but I think they make a girl look better, don't you?"

Adam Joshua was just relieved that it wasn't more hair. He tried to think of other things besides dimples, and still nod enough so that Nelson thought he was listening.

All of a sudden he stopped and stared.

George was heading fast down the sidewalk across the street with a dog Adam Joshua had never seen before.

"That's Lucy," Nelson said as Adam Joshua whistled and tried to get George's attention. "Mr. and Mrs. Sills just got her last week."

George and Lucy disappeared from sight.

Adam Joshua gave a final whistle and gave up.

"One of my fish has dimples too," said Nelson.

———

Since Ms. D wasn't there yet, Martha was

working away in the classroom. Kate had paid her extra, for some extra tattooing.

"NATE'S GREAT!!" Martha was writing on Kate's arm, and she was adding a lot of hearts and flowers and swirling swirls all around it.

Nate stuck his head in around the classroom door.

"Is Kate here yet?" he whispered.

"She's here," Angie told him, grinning. "Getting a tattoo with hearts and flowers and somebody's name."

Nate groaned as he sidled into the room and slipped along to the coatroom.

"I guess we know whose," he muttered.

As soon as her tattoo was finished, Kate looked around the classroom for Nate, and then she looked at the coatroom with a gleam in her eye.

Kate went into it in a hurry, and Nate came out even faster.

"Arghh!" he yelped, wiping his mouth and spitting a lot as he sped past Adam Joshua and Nelson.

When Adam Joshua went to hang his coat in the coatroom, there was a note waiting for him in his cubbyhole.

"I LIKE YOU!" said the note. Instead of a name, it was signed with a little smiling heart.

Adam Joshua had been worrying so much about having to appreciate Elliot, he'd forgotten all about someone getting to appreciate him.

"That's great, Adam Joshua," said Nelson, looking around to see if Gabby was near the coatroom, then sticking a note and a piece of gum into her cubbyhole.

"This might not be such a bad idea after all," Sidney said happily, finding a note and some jelly beans.

There was still some time before class started, and Adam Joshua decided he might as well get appreciating Elliot over with for the day.

He'd been thinking about it a lot, and he'd decided to start with the top of Elliot. If you just looked at Elliot's hair, and you pretended it didn't grow on Elliot, it was nice enough hair.

Adam Joshua took a deep breath.

"You have nice hair," he wrote, and since Elliot wasn't there yet, he scurried over and stuck the note in Elliot's desk.

"Yuck, yuck, yuck, yuck, double yuck!" he muttered, hurrying back again to his own.

———

"Adam Joshua," Martha said, stopping by, "you haven't had a heart tattoo yet."

"Not interested," Adam Joshua said, holding tight to his milk money.

"Adam Joshua," Martha said, "it would

help you get in the mood for Valentine's Day. And look . . ."

Martha's sign had a new note.

"Dogs or cats instead of initials, only five cents more."

Adam Joshua rolled up his sleeve and handed over his money.

"That's a great tattoo, Adam Joshua," Angie said later on her way past. "George looks very nice in a heart."

Angie showed Adam Joshua her arm.

"I had Martha put in a picture of my hamster, Walton Nine. He's been sick a lot lately, and I thought it might help cheer him up.

"It'd better," she sighed. "A hamster in a heart costs five cents more than a dog."

———

Mr. D. got to the classroom before Ms. D., but as soon as he turned around and realized it, he went back and held the classroom door open, then tried to stand far enough out of the way so she could get through.

"Sorry," he told her. "I thought you were right beside me."

"I started out right beside you"—Ms. D. sighed—"but I ended up way behind."

"You're walking for two." Mr. D. said, winking at the class.

"Do you have any money yet?" Martha whispered to Mr. D. before he left.

"I'm saving up," he whispered back.

———

Elliot got there just as the bell rang.

Adam Joshua watched while he read his note.

Elliot smiled and got out his comb and ran it through his hair.

He spent a lot of time on the wave at the front, and he looked around a lot to see if people were paying attention.

Adam Joshua, for one, made sure that Elliot knew he wasn't.

After art, Adam Joshua found a small box of chocolates in his desk.

After recess, he found a lollipop.

When he put on his coat at the end of the day to go home, there was a packet of gumdrops in the pocket.

And every time, there was a tiny card attached with a little heart smiling out at him.

———

"Adam Joshua," Nelson asked, on their way home from school, "have you ever wondered what kissing feels like?"

Adam Joshua tripped over his own foot, banged his knee on a fire hydrant, dropped his book bag, and ended up sitting in the middle of the sidewalk.

Nelson didn't even notice.

"I'm glad you agree," Nelson was saying by the time Adam Joshua caught up with him.

And he waved good-bye as he turned off for his house.

George was lying on the porch across the street looking like he was waiting for someone besides Adam Joshua.

"Hey, George!" Adam Joshua yelled, putting down his book bag and getting ready to catch George.

George turned his head and pretended not to notice.

"George!" Adam Joshua yelled a little louder and a lot madder.

Mrs. Sills opened the door, and Lucy bounced out on the porch to meet George. They took off down the walk and George didn't look back once.

"George!" Adam Joshua yelled after them.

He put a lot about feeling betrayed into it.

CHAPTER 3

"I've been telling my fish a lot about Heidi, Adam Joshua," Nelson said the next morning while they walked.

"I think they're feeling a little jealous," he said. "Especially Cleopatra.

"And I think Jaws and Moby Dick think I'm a little crazy," said Nelson.

Adam Joshua normally couldn't stand Nelson's fish, but he thought he might like to get to know Jaws and Moby a little better.

"They'd probably understand if Heidi was a fish." Nelson sighed.

———

It was hard to get into the coatroom at school because of the crowd.

"Ms. D. got here early to help some kids with makeup work," Angie told Adam Joshua and Nelson, "so Martha's selling her heart tattoos in the coatroom. So far, Ms. D.'s been too busy to notice."

Nelson's eyes lit up the minute he saw that Heidi was in line, waiting for a heart and initials.

"I need the initials in my heart changed," Gabby was telling Martha. "Right now. Right away."

"And I'm going to need two hearts," said Jonesy. "With different initials."

"I need a heart just in case," Tyler said, joining the line. "I'll have the initials added later."

As soon as Martha was finished with their tattoos, people were pulling their sleeves down tight.

"It's five cents extra if you want me to keep quiet," Martha told them.

"Right," everybody sighed, handing over more milk money.

———

Ms. D. left the room for a few minutes, so everyone spilled out of the coatroom and over to the window, where Martha could have more light.

"Excuse me," Nelson told Adam Joshua. "I have to go see Martha about a tattoo."

People who'd already been tattooed, and who hadn't changed their minds yet about the initials they'd been tattooed with, were working on their valentines. Sidney was sending one to Santa Claus.

"It never hurts to keep in touch," he told everybody.

Adam Joshua decided it was probably Elliot appreciation time again.

He'd been thinking about it, but there wasn't much on the way down from Elliot's hair that he cared much for.

"Your shoes are nice," Adam Joshua wrote.

He acted like he'd forgotten something in the coatroom, and he slipped into it and put the note in Elliot's cubbyhole.

There was already something new in his own. "I REALLY REALLY LIKE YOU," the note read, and it was attached to an enormous heart-shaped lollipop.

"Adam Joshua," Angie said, coming in. "You are so lucky. You have the nicest Secret Friend I've ever heard of. All I've gotten from mine so far is half a banana, and a tuna fish sandwich with bites taken out of it. I'm pretty sure," Angie said, glumly, "that I'm just getting pieces of somebody's lunch."

Adam Joshua went back into the classroom

just as Ms. D. was getting everyone settled down for the day's work.

He started math humming a little under his breath.

If you left out anything having to do with Elliot, it could be that Secret Friends were one of Ms. D.'s best ideas yet.

———

Sometime during the morning, Elliot went into the coatroom, and when he came out he was smiling and looking down to admire his shoes.

He spent the rest of the day with his feet sticking out in the middle of the aisle so everyone else could admire his shoes too, but everyone spent most of the day tripping over them instead.

And sometime during the morning, Ms. D. suddenly looked up from her work and said, "Oh, Adam Joshua, I want to apologize to you."

Adam Joshua looked up in surprise, and so did everyone else in the class. Ms. D. didn't need to apologize all that often, and she'd never apologized to him.

"I just wanted to say that I'm sorry no one got to draw your name as a Secret Friend."

Adam Joshua looked more surprised than ever.

"I was tidying up after school yesterday," Ms. D. said, "and I found the slip of paper with your name on it stuck in a crevice at the bottom of the basket. Because Doug's been sick, it came out even and I thought everyone had a name."

"Adam Joshua," Nelson whispered from across the aisle. "If you don't have a Secret Friend, who the heck's been sending you all those notes and things?"

Adam Joshua wasn't sure why, but the thought of the answer to that question made cold prickles gather all the way across the back of his neck.

———

Adam Joshua stayed in during the afternoon recess to finish his valentines. A lot of other people were doing the same.

Sidney was sending one to the President.

"It doesn't hurt to stay in touch with him either," he said. "Besides, I think he talks to Santa Claus."

Every time Adam Joshua drew Superman's 'S' with a picture of George in it, he started worrying about Lucy.

In between he worried about who was sending him Secret Friend stuff and liking him so much when he didn't have a Secret Friend.

He would have worried about Nelson and Heidi with her hair and dimples too, but there was just so much a kid could handle.

Eleanor came out of the coatroom looking

disgusted, and went over to the side chalk-board.

"To my Secret Friend," she wrote. "Get with it! I do not like stupid notes or cheap candy. I do like chocolate, jewelry, and money."

Adam Joshua finished his cards and hurried over to the valentine boxes to deliver them before the rest of the class started coming in again.

Everyone had their names on their boxes. Some people had decided to draw on their symbols too.

Sidney's box had a dragon with an enormous number of teeth, but Adam Joshua had no idea what it symbolized about Sidney.

Martha had drawn an incredibly fancy heart on her box. Inside it was a picture of her snake, Reba.

Kate had drawn a picture of Nate holding

a sign that read, "I LOVE BEAUTIFUL KATE."

Adam Joshua was nearly finished stuffing the boxes, and was whistling along, when he saw something that made him screech to a stop.

Heidi had drawn her symbol on the side of her box too.

And it was a very familiar little smiling heart.

CHAPTER 4

While the rest of the class bustled in after recess, Adam Joshua sat at his desk and worried.

Just because he was getting love notes with smiling hearts, and just because Heidi had a smiling heart on her box, it didn't mean his notes were from Heidi. A lot of people probably drew hearts like that all the time.

"Or it's a joke," he muttered. Philip or Jonesy were great at playing jokes.

The more he thought about it, the more it

seemed like a joke.

Suddenly he felt a lot better.

"Adam Joshua," Nelson whispered. "Look!"

Nate was slipping something into Heidi's desk while Heidi was at the front of the room talking to Ms. D.

"Oh, no!" moaned Nelson. "I know he's not her Secret Friend or anything."

Heidi came back to her desk.

Nate watched Heidi.

Kate watched Nate.

Nelson watched Heidi and Nate.

Adam Joshua watched Heidi and Nate and Kate and Nelson.

Heidi reached into her desk for paper and came out with a little stuffed bear holding a heart in its paws.

"Ohh," she whispered. "I love it. I just love it!"

"Arghh!" Nelson said sadly.

Nate blushed to a nice pink and sat at his

desk looking very pleased, happily humming under his breath. Kate turned fiery red, and there was nearly steam coming out of her ears while she sat banging her foot against her chair.

Heidi handed the bear across the aisle for Angie to see, and Angie handed it to Hanah, and pretty soon it was going all around the classroom, and everybody was saying, "Oh, how cute!" and "Who do you think sent it?"

"Double arghh!" Nelson said, thumping his head on his desktop.

Nate was too embarrassed to look at Heidi, and Kate was too mad, and Nelson was too miserable, which was all just as well. Because Heidi spent the rest of the day beaming across the room at Adam Joshua, flashing a brilliant smile, dimples and all.

———

"Don't forget, tomorrow's Valentine's Day," Ms. D. said as they were all packing up to go home. "As if you would forget." She laughed, looking at the overflowing card boxes.

When Adam Joshua and Nelson went into the coatroom, three people were sitting on top of Nate so that Martha could write "KATE'S GREAT!" on his arm.

Nate's eyes stared at Adam Joshua in a panic, but since Kate had her hand clamped over his mouth, Nate didn't say much.

Adam Joshua and Nelson rescued Nate, but Martha made Kate pay her anyway.

"All that you got written was 'KATE'S GR . . .'" yelped Kate.

"I should charge you extra for the sitting on," muttered Martha.

Tucked way back in Adam Joshua's cubbyhole was another note.

"IT'S MORE THAN LIKE," the note said. "I LOVE YOU."

Adam Joshua went cold all over, and his mouth went dry, and his knees wobbled.

He stuffed everything into his backpack as quickly as he could and left the room in a hurry, not looking at anyone.

Especially Heidi.

———

"I want to go in early tomorrow," Nelson said as they walked home. "I've been thinking about it a lot, and I've decided I'm going to give Heidi a gift."

Adam Joshua didn't think he'd survive Heidi getting any more gifts from anyone.

"I've never given a girl a gift before," Nelson said, "and I never thought I would, but I think I will."

Adam Joshua wondered if there was a way to transfer to a school on the other side of town.

"Well, I guess I have given girls gifts at birthday parties and things," Nelson said, looking thoughtful. "And I give my mother gifts, and she's a girl, sort of."

Adam Joshua wasn't sure the other side of town was far enough away. He might have to go to another state. He'd always heard Alaska was nice, and he was pretty sure they didn't have as many girls there.

"But I've never given a girl a gift for no reason," Nelson said. He walked along quietly beside Adam Joshua for a minute. "I guess I have a reason," he said.

They both sighed.

———

George was waiting when Adam Joshua got home, and personally, Adam Joshua thought it was about time.

"This may be one of the worst days of my life," he began telling George before they even started up the stairs to his room.

There was a scratching at the front door.

When he opened it, Lucy was sitting there, looking disappointed that it had been Adam Joshua, and not George, who'd answered.

"I'm sorry, but he's not here right now," Adam Joshua told Lucy.

Lucy just sat and stared at him.

"Okay," said Adam Joshua. "He's here, but he's busy."

Lucy sat some more and stared some more.

"Very busy," said Adam Joshua. "He wouldn't want to come out now, even if he could come out now, because we're having a talk. Man to man."

Lucy lifted her ears and started to smile.

Adam Joshua was relieved that she was starting to understand about George.

"Well, really it's more boy to dog," he said. "But anyway, he probably won't be around much anymore. We have a lot to talk about."

Lucy's eyes lit up and she smiled ear to ear, which on Lucy was a big smile.

"A lot of what we have to talk over is about girls," Adam Joshua added. "So it will take a

long time. And then I think that we're going to Alaska. But I'll be sure to tell him—"

George streaked out the door between Adam Joshua's legs and headed down the sidewalk with Lucy, and they didn't look back once.

"—that you stopped by," Adam Joshua finished up, closing the door slowly and carefully behind George.

CHAPTER 5

"We never even had a chance to talk about Alaska," Adam Joshua told George the next morning.

Actually, George was sound asleep and couldn't have cared less. He'd come home late the night before without an explanation or a word of apology. He'd been snoring away, exhausted, ever since.

"I was pretty sure we were going to Alaska," Adam Joshua reminded George. "Because of Heidi."

Actually, one of George's favorite things to chew on was Adam Joshua's map book, and he'd chewed Alaska right off the page a long time ago. Adam Joshua had a pretty good idea of where it was, but it wasn't easy on a map with teeth marks to figure out how to get there.

"Now I've got to go to school," Adam Joshua said. "And it's Valentine's Day, and whatever happens is going to happen today, and whatever it is, it's going to be awful."

George snored on.

"Alaska would have been the best idea," Adam Joshua said firmly.

———

Nelson showed up for their school walk carrying a small plastic bag of water with a big red bow on top. A silver sparkly fish was swimming around in it looking depressed.

Adam Joshua couldn't believe it. For as long as he'd known Nelson, he'd been crazy about his fish. Fish had always meant more to Nelson than anything.

Until Heidi.

"Several fish volunteered," Nelson said. "And then the whole aquarium voted that Long John should be the one to go. He loves meeting new people, especially girls, and he's a real party animal."

Adam Joshua didn't think Long John looked a thing like a party animal, but maybe he was the sort of fish that didn't cheer up until the party got going.

"I know she'll love Long John," Nelson said. "If she loved a stuffed bear, just think how she's going to go crazy when she sees a live fish."

Adam Joshua just wished he'd worked a little harder on the Alaska thing.

———

There weren't many people in the room when they got to school.

Martha was setting up her sign and looking exhausted.

"I don't think I've written initials in anybody's heart tattoo that match the initials in anybody else's heart in the entire room," she groaned. "Not that it matters, because everybody keeps having me change the initials they have anyway. But they still never match."

Nelson made Adam Joshua keep watch at the classroom door while he said good-bye to his fish and put the bag in Heidi's desk.

"Long John says he's very excited, Adam Joshua," Nelson said when he was finished. "He says from everything I've told him about Heidi, he thinks he's going to have a really wonderful life."

People started pouring in the door. A lot of them zoomed straight toward Martha, and Martha got a glazed, crazed look in her eye and moaned loudly.

Heidi came in next, talking to Angie. She had on a red sweater and had red heart barrettes in her hair, and as she passed Adam Joshua's desk, she laid a candy heart on it that said, "HI, CUTIE!"

Nelson looked really puzzled.

"Adam Joshua," he said, "why on earth would she do that?"

Heidi wandered around a lot before she settled down.

Every time she wandered near her desk, Nelson held his breath.

Every time she wandered away again, Nelson sighed.

Finally, Heidi sat down at her desk and reached into it, getting ready to get down to business.

Nelson's eyes lit up, and his face lit up, and his whole body lit up watching Heidi.

"She's going to love it, Adam Joshua," Nelson whispered. "She's just going to go *nuts*!"

He was absolutely, positively, totally right.

For the next several minutes, Heidi went nuts.

First she screamed and jumped out of her chair, and then she screamed again for good measure.

Nelson let out a little scream himself.

"A fish!" hollered Heidi. "A fish! Who on earth would put a fish in my desk?!"

Nelson's eyes got big, and he looked terrified.

"Everybody knows how much I hate fish!" Heidi yelled. "Everybody knows it's the one thing in the whole world I really can't stand."

Nelson looked at Adam Joshua in a panic.

"This is the meanest thing anybody's ever done to me," Heidi said, bursting into tears and running from the room, holding the bag with Long John in it out at arm's length.

Angie and Hanah ran after her.

Everybody in the class froze in their tracks,

got quiet, and stayed quiet, waiting to see what would happen.

Nelson slumped down in his chair, looking totally collapsed.

"Adam Joshua," he whispered. "What went wrong?"

Sidney walked in the room, looked around at all the quiet and looked puzzled, then checked the number on the door to make sure he was in the right class.

Angie came back and stood in the doorway with her hands on her hips.

"Well," Angie said, glaring at all of them, "I hope whoever did that really feels ashamed of himself. That was the meanest trick I've ever seen. The worst day that ever happened to Heidi had a fish in it."

Everybody, even the people who didn't do anything and who had no idea what was going on, looked ashamed.

Sidney hung his head and walked guiltily to his desk.

"How bad a day could it have been?" Philip snickered.

Angie looked like she was getting ready to bop Philip.

"Er," said Philip, clearing his throat and trying to look more interested. "What happened to this fish?"

"Well, what do you think?" Angie said, looking at him suspiciously. "She flushed it."

———

For the rest of the morning, Nelson sat at his desk and moaned and groaned softly and looked terrible.

Heidi sat at her desk sniffling, except somewhere toward late morning she started looking a whole lot madder than upset, and Nelson started looking really scared.

"I'm really going to get whoever did that,"

Heidi growled once when Ms. D. stepped out of the room.

Adam Joshua could see Nelson shaking in his chair from clear across the aisle.

CHAPTER 6

Some people went outside after lunch. Some people went back to the classroom. Some people panicked and decided they'd better get started on their valentines, since it was nearly time for everyone to open them.

Heidi, Angie, and Hanah went all over the playground asking suspicious-looking people questions about fish.

Nelson had calmed down a little during lunch, although it was too bad it had been fish sticks. Now he just sat at his desk and looked miserably sad, but Adam Joshua didn't know if it was for Heidi or Long John.

Adam Joshua and several other guys all chipped in to help pay Martha so she'd finish what she'd started tatooing on Nate's arm.

"KATE'S GRUESOME!!" they had her write.

A lot of people were sneaking around leaving gifts for their Secret Friends since Valentine's Day was the last day to do it.

Adam Joshua was all out of Elliot parts. There was nothing left he could say he liked without saying he liked Elliot.

He couldn't stand Elliot. Still, even Elliot probably needed to have more than just his shoes and hair appreciated.

He had a lot of the candy left that Heidi had given him, and all things considered, he didn't feel much like eating it. He got the big lollipop, took the smiling heart note off, and added one of his own.

"There are a lot of things about you to appreciate," he wrote, gritting his teeth.

Ms. D. had said they could each decide whether to tell their Secret Friend who they were or not.

"Absolutely not," Adam Joshua muttered, sticking the lollipop in Elliot's desk.

———

Elliot found his lollipop when he came in, and he read the note and looked so pleased with himself, Adam Joshua started to worry that he'd start singing about it or something.

He laid the lollipop out on his desk so that everyone could see it, and Adam Joshua saw him pat the note twice.

———

Mr. D. dropped in during the afternoon just as they were getting ready to start their class party.

"For you," he told Ms. D., making a grand,

sweeping bow, and handing her a terrific bouquet of flowers.

Everybody cheered and applauded, and Mr. D. turned toward them and took another bow.

"Don't encourage him," Ms. D. said, laughing.

Normally, when Mr. D. kissed Ms. D., everybody looked somewhere else, or they closed their eyes, or they moaned and groaned.

Today, Adam Joshua noticed that everybody seemed to be watching closely, and some people seemed to be moving their lips right along.

———

When they opened their boxes of valentines, the first thing everybody did was to check for candy. Then they counted to make sure everyone had given them a card.

"Hey, there's one missing!" Eleanor yelped. "I've got a checklist," she said, "and as soon as I figure out the symbols, whoever didn't give me a card is going to be in big trouble."

Everyone panicked for a minute, trying to remember and make sure they hadn't forgotten Eleanor.

Then they got down to the business of opening cards and trying to guess the symbols.

Angie had signed her valentines with the drawing of a fairly sick-looking hamster.

"I would have made him look healthy," she said, "but then I wasn't sure anybody would know the cards were from me."

"I'm glad you're my friend," she'd written to Adam Joshua.

Elliot Banks had signed his valentines with a $.

"What else?" he said smugly.

He'd given Adam Joshua a black valentine and had drawn skulls and crossbones all over it.

Nobody could figure out Adam Joshua's symbol.

"Superdog?" asked Angie. "Who's Superdog?"

"Maybe it's a dog whose name begins with an 'S'?" Martha asked.

"Does anybody have a dog named Sam or Sid or anything?" asked Jonesy.

Heidi had signed her card with the little smiling heart.

"Adam Joshua," she'd written, "would you like to go steady?"

And when Adam Joshua looked up, Heidi was watching him read it.

"I want to talk to you after school," she called over to him.

Angie opened her next card. "A fish?" she

said, chuckling. "Who could it be but Nelson?"

"Nelson?" said Heidi. "I forgot all about Nelson and fish!"

Nelson looked up and listened in, and started looking a little worried.

"Nobody's as crazy about fish as Nelson," said Hanah.

They all turned to look at Nelson suspiciously.

"That rat!" Heidi yelped. "That really rotten, absolute rat!"

Nelson went from looking worried to terrified in a second.

"I want to talk to you after school too," Heidi growled at him from across the room.

Angie and Hanah nodded solemnly.

———

Mr. D. went to get a tattoo from Martha when Ms. D. wasn't looking.   .

"Honestly," Ms. D. said, catching them at

it. "I don't know which one of you is worse."

"He is," Martha said, finishing up with a flourish.

"I paid extra," Mr. D. said proudly, showing Ms. D. his tattoo. "But I think it was worth it."

Martha had drawn a big heart that said "Ms. D." Then she'd drawn a tiny little smiling heart inside it that just said "Baby."

"Absolutely worth it," Ms. D. said, laughing. "Every single cent."

———

"Valentine's Day is over for another year," Ms. D. said sadly, as they all gathered up cards and candy to head home.

"Thank goodness!" at least half the class and Martha said.

Adam Joshua and Nelson offered to help Mr. D. carry things to the car for Ms. D. so they could make it outside with a bodyguard.

"Nelson, I don't know what you did to

those girls," Mr. D. said, watching as Heidi, Angie, and Hanah followed. "But I'd say they were about ready to boil you in oil."

Adam Joshua personally thought Nelson would be lucky to get off that easily.

"And Adam Joshua," Mr. D. whispered, "when Heidi's not glaring at Nelson, she's beaming at you. I can't figure out which one of you she's after first."

Adam Joshua wondered if Mr. D. knew anything about Alaska.

"Well, I'll hold them off at the pass," Mr. D. said, "so you two can make a getaway now. But you're on your own after that."

Mr. D. asked the girls to go in and help him with some more things, and they didn't look any too happy about it, but they went.

And Adam Joshua and Nelson made the fastest getaway they'd ever got in their lives.

———

They weren't very far down the sidewalk

before Nate went screeching by with Kate right behind.

Nelson didn't even notice.

"There's nothing sadder than a dead fish, Adam Joshua," he said as they walked. "I usually have a funeral when one of my fish dies. I always tell all the good things I loved about that fish, and then I say a prayer I learned about fish, and I put a flower on the grave, and I play my bugle."

Nate and Kate went back by, and Adam Joshua was sorry to see that Kate was gaining fast.

"Usually the fish has to be there to be buried," Nelson said, looking worried. "But it's not Long John's fault he can't be there, so I'll just have to do the best I can without him."

There was a terrible scream from Nate, but Adam Joshua didn't even bother to turn around and look back. It seemed to him it was every guy for himself by now.

"Maybe I could just draw a picture of Long John and bury that." Nelson sighed glumly.

———

George wasn't home. Adam Joshua wasn't surprised.

He went on up to his room and started to do a lot of thinking. It wasn't easy without a dog to do it with.

After a while, Adam Joshua could see Nelson outside playing his bugle beside his fish graveyard. A row of rocks was lined up on the ground, each with the name of a fish and a date.

George and Lucy had stopped by for the funeral.

They were sitting, listening politely and looking sad.

Adam Joshua watched for a while, and then he got his map book and studied the world through George's teeth marks. Finally

he gave up, got out a piece of paper, and wrote a note.

"Dear Heidi," he wrote. "I'm the one who gave you the fish."

And he signed it with his name instead of with his Superman-George symbol so she wouldn't have any doubt at all about who it was from.